CABIN CREEK MYSTERIES

THE BLIZZARD ON BLUE MOUNTAIN

THE BLIZZARD ON BLUE MOUNTAIN

by Kristiana Gregory

Illustrated by Patrick Faricy

SCHOLASTIC INC.

New York Toronto London Auckland Sydney
Mexico City New Delhi Hong Kong Buenos Aires

ISBN-13: 978-0-545-00379-7
ISBN-10: 0-545-00379-2

Text copyright © 2008 by Kristiana Gregory
Illustrations copyright © 2008 by Scholastic Inc.
"David's Map" illustration by Cody Rutty.

12 11 10 9 8 7 6 5 4 3 2 1   9 10 11 12 13 14/0

Printed in the U.S.A.   40

First printing, February 2009

CHAPTERS

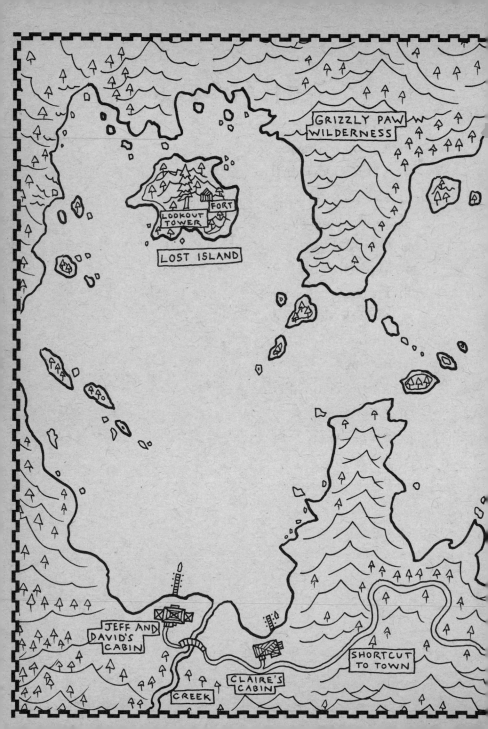

1

A Lost Key

Ten-year-old David Bridger dug in the pockets of his ski parka. He could feel coins, gum wrappers, and parts of a sandwich, but no key. His older brother, Jeff, stood beside him in the snow, worried. They were at the chalet, halfway up Blue Mountain. On weekends and during school breaks, the boys helped out in the cafeteria with their cousin, Claire Posey. In exchange, the three children received free lift tickets and a free lunch.

"Where else could you have put it?" Jeff asked. "We're going to be in so much trouble if you've lost another one."

"It was here a minute ago," David said. He glanced around the deck where skiers were having picnics and enjoying the sunshine. There was a pleasant aroma of wood smoke from an outdoor barbecue.

"I took the snow shovel back to the shed," David explained, "and unlocked the door. Then I set the key on the railing while I put things away. Same as last time."

Jeff was twelve and wanted to set a good example. He had brown hair and sensitive brown eyes. He showed his younger brother the string around his neck, which held an identical key: It, too, opened the shed and the cafeteria's back door. "See, this is how I keep mine safe. Miss Allen said she'll take away our ski passes if one more thing goes missing."

"I know, I *know*. Help me find it, please?"

The brothers retraced David's path from the shed to the cafeteria. They checked the lost and found. Again, they searched pockets. But there was no key.

"Now what?" David asked. His blue eyes looked worried. He yanked off his knit cap, revealing blond hair sticking every which way.

Jeff sighed. "I don't know. Let's think about this for a minute."

Beyond the sundeck was a control booth for the ski lift. The motor was loud. It clicked and groaned as it rolled the dangling chairs uphill like a giant pulley. The brothers looked longingly at the slope where the chairs continued to the top of the mountain. They had hoped to go snowboarding with Claire after finishing their chores.

"I hate being in trouble," David said. He saw a french fry that a kid had dropped, and tossed it to some tiny birds pecking the ground — mountain chickadees. But a large gray jay that had been watching from a pine tree swooped down and snatched the fry. It flew away with it dangling from its beak like a worm.

"We're not supposed to feed wild animals!" called Claire from the cafeteria doorway. She was only nine, but she liked to supervise her older cousins. She had green eyes and red hair, which she usually wore pulled back in a pony-tail like today. A chef's apron was over her jeans and sweater. She went to the brothers with a concerned look.

"Guys, did you take a bag of potato chips from the kitchen?"

The boys looked at each other. "Huh?" they said.

She put her hands on her hips. "Don't tease me."

"What're you talking about?" Jeff asked. "We've been shoveling snow."

Claire frowned. "Miss Allen is mad at me. I left the back door open for a minute, because the kitchen was so hot. There were ten little bags on the shelf, but when I turned around, there were only nine. It happened yesterday, too. I thought you guys probably just forgot to sign out for them. You always get chips with your burgers."

"Wasn't us, Claire. Sorry."

When David told her about his key, Claire lowered herself to a bench.

"We're doomed," she said, shaking her head. "Miss Allen's not going to trust us anymore now that we've lost two keys."

The boys sat beside her. They watched the slope where several kids on snowboards were swirling downhill. They were dressed in bright jackets and baggy snow pants. As they raced by the sundeck on their way to the bottom of the mountain, they waved to the cousins.

"There go our friends," David said. "What are we going to do all winter if we lose our ski passes? By the time we earn enough money to buy new ones, it'll be summer."

Jeff was quiet. He had a lump in his throat remembering the last time their father had taken them snowboarding. It was a year ago.

The following day, he and another forest ranger had died in an avalanche. The brothers liked being outdoors — especially in the snow — because it made them feel closer to their dad.

"Maybe Miss Allen will give us another chance," Claire said. "Let's go talk to her."

But just then Miss Allen marched across the deck. She wore dainty boots with fur around her ankles and skinny pants. "I need to have a word with you children," she said.

She showed them her wrist. Her sleeve was rolled up.

"My watch is missing," she said. "I took it off to scrub some dishes and set it on the windowsill. Now it's gone. This is the last straw. Since you're the only kids with keys to the kitchen, I'm holding you responsible. I'm taking your passes away."

2

Another Chance

Miss Allen's office was in the chalet next to the kitchen.

"I like you kids," she said. She was holding their passes, looking at their photo IDs. "You're hard workers, you're polite. And last summer you solved that mystery at the Blue Mountain Lodge —" She bit her lip, then looked out the window at the ski slope.

The cousins knew she was talking about an employee who had been taken to jail.

Miss Allen had been a manager at the Lodge when some historic heirlooms were stolen.

"Kids, I'm new at this job. The owners, the Zimmermans, will fire me if customers aren't happy or if food disappears. And if I report my missing watch — well, I don't want people to think there's a thief here. You *must* be more responsible and keep strangers out of the kitchen."

Miss Allen drummed her fingers on her desk, thinking. After a long moment, she handed the children's passes back to them.

"Here's what I'm going to do," she said. "This place is swarming with families on vacation for their winter break. I need your help cleaning tables and so forth during the lunch hour. Eat what you want. Just make sure you continue to mark the chart — every burger, every pickle, every soda. You get the idea. This way I can keep track of things. But" — she pointed a manicured finger at them — "if any customers complain about you, or if anything else disappears from the kitchen, you'll be spending the rest of your winter in town."

"Miss Allen, you can count on us," Jeff said. David and Claire nodded in agreement. They kept silent about David having lost a second key.

She smiled at the children. "One last thing," she said. "As you know, I'm upset about my watch. My mother gave it to me when I graduated from high school. It's engraved with both our names. Maybe you kids can solve that mystery, too."

David whispered as they left Miss Allen's office, "What if someone found both my keys?"

"That might explain her missing watch," Claire replied.

In a low voice, Jeff said, "Then we've really got to keep an eye on this place."

The cousins were so glad to have their jobs back, they wanted to give Miss Allen extra help. They decided to wait until later in the afternoon to go snowboarding.

David swept around the four-sided fireplace in the center of the cafeteria. Jeff picked up trash and mopped the kitchen floor. A large pan of brownies that had been cooling by an open kitchen window was

Claire's responsibility. She cut the brownies into forty-eight servings. Then, one by one, she put them in cellophane and tied them with a blue ribbon. They would sell for one dollar apiece at the dessert counter.

"I'll take one of those," Jeff said when he hung up the mop.

"Me, too!" said David, setting his broom in the corner. "I love these things. I'll write our names on the chart. Want one, Claire?"

"Yep. Then leave them on this shelf. Miss Allen said she'll put them out front when she makes the afternoon coffee."

Jeff bit into his brownie. "Mm, yum. This is awesome," he said. "Two whole weeks of no school and free food."

"I can't wait to hit the slopes!" David cried.

A small room off the kitchen held the cousins' gear and warm clothes. After zipping their snow pants over their jeans and putting on their boots, they carried their boards out into the cold sunshine. Their season passes hung from their necks. While they were standing in the lift line, two women on skis slid up behind them.

"The cafeteria is a pigsty," one said to the other. "There was spilled ketchup all over one of the tables. We couldn't find a clean place to sit."

"The same thing happened to us," said the other woman. "We've been coming here for years, but it's never been this bad."

Claire shot a look of alarm at her cousins. "I thought you guys cleaned up," she said in a low voice.

"Jeff was supposed to do the tables," said David, moving forward in line with his snowboard on one foot.

"No way. That was your job. I mopped the kitchen floor."

"But, Jeff, you were the one with a bucket. All I had was a broom —"

"Maybe we should go back," Claire interrupted.

But just then it was the cousins' turn to get on the lift. The three-person chair going uphill slowed to where they were standing and dipped low enough for them to sit down.

"It's too late to turn around now!" Jeff cried as the cousins lowered the safety bar that provided a footrest. The chair swayed with their weight, then straightened out as it began its ascent. It would take eight minutes to get to the top of Blue Mountain.

Claire turned around to see the women behind them, but the height made her dizzy. She quickly faced forward again.

"Did you hear that?" she asked her cousins without looking at them.

"What?"

"We gotta beat those ladies downhill," Claire said. "They're so mad about the dirty tables, they're going straight to Miss Allen to complain."

3

A Race Downhill

Eight minutes on the lift seemed like an hour to the cousins. When they reached the top, they slid off the moving chair and over to a ridge. The view was magnificent: blue sky and a panorama of snowy peaks. The town of Cabin Creek was nestled at the base of Blue Mountain.

"Ready?" Jeff asked his companions. He snapped on his helmet and adjusted his goggles.

"Ready," said David, doing the same.

Claire's purple helmet sparkled in the sunlight. "I'll be right behind you, guys."

The next chair rolling up the lift carried the two women. Just as the women got off, the cousins launched themselves down the slope.

The boys' dad had taught them to always ski in control, and to be courteous to others.

But today, David was in a hurry. Soon he was ahead of his brother and Claire, swinging his hips — arms out to balance himself — carving the slope with sprays of snow. He lifted his heels to jump.

"Let's catch some air!" he cried.

"Hey, kid!" yelled a man on skis. He was wearing a sleek black jumpsuit with a red fanny pack. "Watch where you're going or I'll report all of you!"

"Sorry, mister!" David waved to the man but, as he did, he tripped. His board slammed into a mogul — a large, icy bump — which sent him flying. In a sprawl, he landed face-down, sliding off the trail into soft snow. He lay there trying to catch his breath.

"You all right, buddy?" Jeff called, hurrying to his younger brother.

Claire came to a smooth stop beside them. "David, you were too wild," she said.

They helped him up. As David coughed slush out of his mouth, the two women skied gracefully past them, planting their poles and turning with ease.

"They're gonna beat us!" David cried, brushing snow from his arms and chest.

"Race you!" said Jeff.

"Hey, guys, we've still got to be careful!" Claire called.

Once again the cousins headed down the mountain. Around the bend, they could see the lunch chalet. Already, the women were removing their skis. They stood them upright in a snowdrift with their poles, where others had done the same. This mound of snow looked like a colorful porcupine.

"Hurry, guys," Jeff said as he swooshed alongside the deck, then up to the kitchen's back door. The cousins unclamped their bindings, stepped out of their snowboards, and rushed inside.

Claire filled a pail with hot, soapy water while the brothers found rags. Soon they were washing tables. They kept glancing out the wide windows that looked onto the slope. The women were talking to friends on the sundeck, gradually making their way toward the cafeteria.

"Here they come," said Jeff. "David, let's go greet 'em."

Claire went to the kitchen and dumped the pail of water into the large sink. As she hung the rags on a hook to dry, she noticed the basket of brownies. It was still on the shelf, but one had fallen onto the counter below.

"That's weird," she said to herself. She picked it up, then counted them. "Hmm. Forty-four. I wrapped up forty-eight. Since we all ate one, there should be forty-five."

David burst into the kitchen with good news. "Those ladies aren't going to complain to Miss Allen," he said. "We showed them all the clean tables and we apologized."

"Yeah," said Jeff. "They were really cool about it. Especially when we told them we're learning on the job. Claire? What's the matter?"

Claire was counting the brownies again. "One's missing," she said. "And no one signed out for it. We've got to put a dollar in the dessert jar before Miss Allen finds out. It wouldn't be right for us to pretend we ate it ourselves."

Jeff scowled. "What's going on here? Someone's taking bags of chips. Miss Allen's watch is missing, David's key, and now a brownie."

"Why would a thief take only one brownie?" David wondered. "I would take a bunch. I mean, if I stole things. Which I would never do."

"I don't get it." Claire was looking around the kitchen. "Nothing is messed up. Maybe some kid snuck back here while we were out. Miss Allen might have been on the phone or something."

David had been searching his pockets. "Here's fifty-five cents," he said, showing them his coins. "What've you got, Jeff?"

"A bunch of nickels," the older boy answered. Together they came up with a dollar, then dropped their coins into the large glass jar with the sign, BLUE MOUNTAIN BROWNIES, ONE BUCK.

Just as the last nickel clinked in, they saw Miss Allen coming through the cafeteria in her fancy boots.

"That was close," said Jeff.

But as they headed out for the slopes, they saw the skier in the black jumpsuit. He was talking to the lift operator, pointing to the cousins.

"Is that guy reporting me?" David asked.

"I hope not," his brother replied. "We sure don't need any more trouble."

"Guys, let's go. I have a bad feeling," said Claire. The man's crimson fanny pack reminded her of the red spot on a black widow spider.

4

The Litterbug

Minutes later, the cousins were on the chair-lift. They kept glancing behind them, hoping the man in black wasn't also riding up.

At the top of the mountain, they again stood on the ridge. This time they looked down the other side to Camp Whispering Pines. The cabins there were deserted for the winter except for the caretaker's, which had smoke curling from its chimney.

A trail connecting the camp to the lunch chalet cut across the lower half of the mountain. The children snowboarded down to this trail, their favorite place to rest. While they were enjoying the view, Claire noticed a blue object in the snow, a few feet away.

"Guys, see that?" She slid over to it, and picked up a blue ribbon. Nearby, she found some cellophane.

"Is that what I think it is?" Jeff asked.

"Yep!" she said. "It's from a brownie. See the crumbs stuck to it?"

"How'd it get way up here?" David questioned. "Miss Allen is probably just now putting them out with the fresh coffee."

"Maybe it's the one that was missing," said Jeff. He studied the tracks along the woodsy trail leading to Camp Whispering Pines. Most of the prints were blurred from all the skis and snowboards that had passed by. But there was no mistaking one of them: It was the size of a cafeteria tray, oval in shape, and it was cross-hatched like a waffle.

"Snowshoes!" Jeff cried. "Probably from Mr. Johnny, the caretaker. He comes this way to work on the lifts, and to see Miss Allen. She's his sister."

"Then maybe he doesn't have to sign out for food," said David. "Wouldn't that explain the missing brownie? And maybe the missing potato chips? He probably just littered by accident."

Claire put the ribbon and cellophane in her pocket to throw away later. "Yeah, but what about your key and Miss Allen's watch? Where did *they* go?"

The cousins wondered about this as they headed down the slope. When they reached the chalet, they saw a pair of snowshoes by the kitchen door.

"Hey, Mr. Johnny's here!" Jeff said, sliding to a stop. "Let's see what we can find out."

Miss Allen and Mr. Johnny were at the long wooden table in the kitchen, eating chili and corn bread. They were laughing, seeming to enjoy each other's company. He was wearing suspenders over a thick, wool sweater. His beard and mussed-up hair made him look like a mountain man.

"Hello, children," said Miss Allen. "Come warm yourselves. My brother just hiked here from camp and is thawing out his feet."

The cousins settled at the table with cups of cocoa. Claire was careful with her question. "Do you like chocolate, Mr. Johnny?"

"I could eat it for breakfast, lunch, and dinner," he answered as he buttered his corn bread. He took a large bite.

"Then you probably like brownies," David said.

Mr. Johnny's mouth was full, but he nodded.

"We like them, too," said Jeff. He wasn't sure how to ask the man if he had signed out for one.

Just then a woman in a red ski patrol parka came into the kitchen with her thermos. "I've really had it with all these kids on vacation," she said to no one in particular.

"What's wrong?" asked Miss Allen.

"It's my first aid pouch," she answered. "I hang it outside, on the railing of the ski patrol hut, so I can grab it in a hurry. I keep my lunch in it. Anyway, for three days now, someone has opened the Velcro straps and swiped stuff. First, a donut was missing, and then yesterday, my bag of trail mix was gone. Today, a ham sandwich. It really ticks me off." She filled her thermos from the hot water spigot, then twisted on the cork. "Well, at least I can make some instant soup. Thank you, Miss Allen."

When the woman left, Miss Allen turned to the cousins. She was no longer smiling. "Do you children know anything about this?"

"No!" they insisted.

"We went by the hut, but we didn't stop," Jeff said.

"That's part of the problem," said Miss Allen. "Whenever something turns up missing, you kids are nearby. If the Zimmermans hear about this —" She glanced at Mr. Johnny, but said no more. He kept his eyes on his bowl of chili, as if he hadn't heard their conversation.

"We better go," Claire said, getting up from the table. While she and the brothers rinsed their cups at the sink, Miss Allen glared at them.

"Remember," she said. "I've warned you."

Outside, the cousins readied their snowboards and goggles for their third and final run.

"That was totally weird in there," Claire said.

"You're not kidding," said Jeff. "Mr. Johnny acted suspicious, but why? And how did that brownie end up on the trail to his cabin? That's what I want to know."

"Me, too," said David. "Let's go to town. I think it's time to bring Sophie the Sleuth into this case."

5

Snow Sleuths

The cousins snowboarded down to the bottom of the hill to Blue Mountain Lodge. Inside was a grand stone fireplace with a real buffalo head over the mantel. Floor-to-ceiling windows looked out at the slopes. Guests were gathered among comfortable chairs and sofas, reading or playing games. The cousins loved hanging out here. There was a pleasant murmur of voices and the aroma of fresh coffee coming from the lunch counter.

"I wonder what Sophie will think about our mystery," David said as they warmed themselves by the fire. They had carried their boards to the lodge basement where their cross-country gear was also stored. During winter, they often skied home through the woods. The cousins' cabins were on the remote shore of the frozen lake, but their new friend, Sophie Garcia, lived in town. The four children often visited back and forth.

"Before we go to her place, we should check in with my mom," said Claire.

Jeff agreed. "It's four o'clock," he said. "It'll be dark soon."

They grabbed their backpacks, which rattled with their flashlights, walkie-talkies, candy, and other supplies. Outside, they passed the ice rink, then walked a few blocks to the

Western Café, which was owned by Claire's parents. Aunt Lilly hugged the boys and her daughter when they came in the door. She had the same red hair and green eyes as Claire. Uncle Wyatt waved to them from behind the grill. He was wearing his favorite cowboy hat.

"Your mother is working late," Aunt Lilly told the boys, "so you can ride home with us in an hour or so. Meantime, here's ten dollars. She'd like you to stop at the market for some carrots and lettuce to make a salad for dinner."

The boys' mother was Dr. Daisy Bridger, Cabin Creek's veterinarian. As long as the children asked their parents' permission and stayed in touch with them, they were allowed to roam the small mountain town.

They left the café, passed the library and animal hospital, turned down Elm Street, then around the corner to Maple. When they came to a cottage with blinking Christmas lights, they went up the path and gave the secret knock: four quick raps followed by four slow ones.

The door flung open. "Hi, guys!" a nine-year-old girl greeted them. "Come on in."

Sophie Garcia had long brown hair and wore a red sweatshirt with jeans. She led the cousins into a living room messy with toy trucks and puzzles. Identical twin boys, three years old, were jumping on the couch. Midair, they waved to the visitors.

"Hey there, Reid. Hi, Robbie," the cousins said. As usual, they and the twins gave one another high fives.

The house had the good baking smell of ginger. Mrs. Garcia was on her laptop in the dining room. The table was stacked with books, magazines, and papers from the antique shop she and her husband owned. "Nice to see you kids again," she said, giving them a warm smile. Her brown hair was loose over her shoulders. "Help yourselves to the cookies cooling on the counter."

"Thank you, Mrs. Garcia!"

With handfuls of ginger snaps, the foursome crowded into Sophie's cluttered room. Her piano was under a window. The sheet music she had been practicing was clothespinned to the curtain. David sat on the piano bench, Jeff on the bed; the girls shared a beanbag chair on the floor.

"Now, down to business," Claire began. While the cousins described the problems up at the lunch chalet, David jotted them down in the sketchbook he always kept in his pack. He drew pictures of the missing items and the skier in the black jumpsuit.

"Very odd," Sophie said, reading his list. "First, David's key vanishes. Then a bag of potato chips — twice. Then Miss Allen's watch. A brownie disappears but you find its ribbon and plastic on the trail to Camp Whispering Pines. A man who reminds you of a black widow spider yells at you guys. And someone steals food from the ski patrol lady, three days in a row."

Sophie closed her eyes, thinking. "Hmm. Except for the key and watch, and that man, I'd say our culprit is hungry."

"Well, we've got to figure this out fast," Claire said. "Before Miss Allen takes away our lift passes and before our good reputation is ruined. We don't want people to think we're thieves. Or that we're irresponsible. And it would be terrible if the Zimmermans fire Miss Allen."

"I see your dilemma," Sophie said. "What's our next move?"

Jeff took the ten dollars from his pocket. "Right now we're on our way to the store. Want to come?"

"I'll get my jacket," Sophie answered. "I need some M&M'S."

Cabin Creek Grocery was on Main Street in one of the town's oldest buildings. The wooden floors creaked as the children walked down the aisles toward the fresh vegetables. They were surprised to see Mr. Johnny in the health food section. He was scooping flour from a bin into a plastic bag.

"Hello," they said to him.

Startled, the man put the bag behind his back. He set it in his cart, then stood in front of it as if to hide it.

"Are you snowshoeing to your cabin tonight?" David asked. He was trying to be friendly.

"Uh . . . no," Mr. Johnny answered. He scratched his beard for a moment, then backed up, pushing his cart toward the cashier. "I'm staying with my sister. I have to work on the chairlift tomorrow morning. Gotta go. See you kids later."

At the checkout stand, Mr. Johnny kept glancing over his shoulder at the children. He paid for his groceries, then hurried away.

The four sleuths gave one another quizzical looks.

"Did Mr. Johnny seem nervous to you?" Jeff asked.

"Definitely."

"Wonder why?"

Sophie crossed her arms and nodded. "He reminds me of my little brothers when they're doing something they shouldn't."

6

A Long Drop

The next day Sophie and Claire rode the chair-lift together. They were wearing goggles to protect their eyes from the bright sunshine, and helmets. Jeff and David were waiting for them up at the lunch chalet. Though Sophie's grandparents had bought her a season pass, she liked helping her friends with chores — especially now that they would be searching for clues.

The girls' snowboards were on the footrest, their hands on the safety bar across their laps. As the chair passed between the frosted trees, skiers swished below them. Orange flags on one of the slopes marked a slalom course where racers were practicing.

"I love living in the mountains," Sophie said. Her family had recently moved from Green Valley, and she was still getting used to riding the lift. "Want some M&M'S?" she asked.

"No, thanks," Claire answered. But before she could warn Sophie not to wiggle around, the girl had removed her gloves and was digging in her pocket. As she did, she slid sideways on the seat and dropped a glove. When she looked down, she bumped her head on the bar, knocking off her helmet — which had not been fastened — and her goggles. She tried to grab them, but dropped her other glove, too.

"Oh, no!" Sophie cried. She watched her sparkly white helmet bounce, then roll down the slope, gathering speed like a snowball. Her gloves had landed near a tree.

Heights made Claire dizzy. It scared her to look down, but she could see that her friend was slipping off the chair. She grabbed her arm, trying to help her scoot backward, but Sophie's sleeve had caught on a jagged piece of metal.

When Sophie realized she couldn't move her arm, she began to panic. She twisted around to grab the back, but as she did, her snowboard slid off the footrest. Now the weight of it was pulling her forward, toward the edge of her seat.

"Claire, I'm falling!" Her brown hair was blowing over her face.

"Hang on, Sophie, don't let go!"

Their chair thumped over the wheels of a tower as it rolled upward. And as it did, Claire felt herself sliding. Quick as she could, she, too, twisted to grab behind her. Now both girls were on their stomachs, heading up the mountain backward, their legs dangling in the air. Their snowboards felt heavier by the moment.

"What's going to happen to us?" Sophie whimpered.

Claire tried to keep the terror out of her voice. "The lift operators will help. We're almost to the lunch chalet." She glanced over her shoulder at the control booth farther up the hill. But the two college boys inside were not looking out the windows, as they should have been. Instead they were laughing and punching each other.

Claire's fingers ached. She took a deep breath. Then she dug her elbows into the slatted seat and boosted herself a few inches. This helped her to tighten her grasp. She felt sorry to see Sophie's bare hands squeezing the cold metal.

Suddenly, Claire noticed a crack in the bar where they were clinging. Scotch tape was wrapped around its sharp edge and around a torn piece of paper. Her heart started racing.

They were riding a broken chair! Claire had seen damaged ones before, but they were always flagged with a sign so no one would get on. Someone had ripped the warning off this one.

Who would do such a thing? But she couldn't think about that now: The bar was bending from their weight, pulling away from the seat.

Claire looked down. It was a long drop to the snow. If they fell, they would suffer terrible injuries. She cast another dizzying look over her shoulder. The control booth was getting closer, its motor a loud rumble.

"Claire, my hands are numb. What if I can't keep —?"

"Any minute now, Sophie. Let's count to ten. One . . . two . . ."

Someone was screaming their names. "Hang on!" Jeff and David were running from the sundeck toward them. The chair was about to reach the landing patch, where skiers would be able to slide off if they weren't continuing up the hill. The brothers could see that Sophie's arm was caught.

"We'll help you!" Jeff yelled. "A few more feet and you're there! Ready . . . now!"

Together, Jeff and David grabbed Sophie by the waist, pulling her out of her jacket. She landed in an awkward sprawl. When Claire felt her foot touch the ground, she let go and ducked so the chair wouldn't hit her as it went by.

Just then the boys in the tower saw the commotion and hit the emergency button.

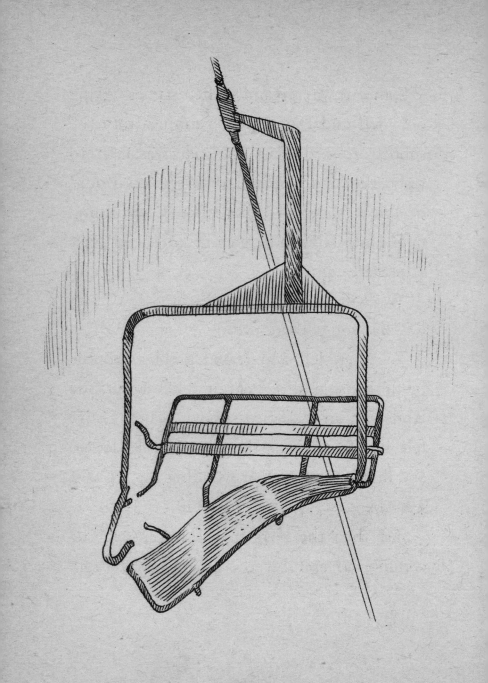

The lift stopped. The broken chair swung from the cable, Sophie's torn coat flapping overhead.

"What's going on here!" a ski patrol man thundered as he clumped over in his heavy boots. He whipped off his sunglasses.

The older boys started pointing and shoving each other. "These girls were fooling around —"

"You're fired!" the man said. "There's no excuse. Turn in your badges. You'll never work on this mountain again. Are you okay, girls?" he asked, helping them step out of their bindings. He carried their snowboards to the deck where there was a ski rack.

Claire felt sick to her stomach and thought she might enjoy a good cry if she were alone in her room. "I've been better," she managed to say.

Sophie was trembling. Though she had lost her helmet and goggles, her gloves and her jacket, she tried to be brave. "Maybe some cocoa will comfort me."

As the kids headed for the chalet, they all wondered the same thing: *Had someone planned for Claire and Sophie to be on that broken chair?*

They became even more uneasy when they saw the man in the black ski suit. He was at one of the picnic tables talking on a cell phone. Though his sunglasses hid his eyes, the children knew he was staring at them.

7
More Trouble

The lift was shut down while workers removed the dangerous chair, and a patrol man brought Sophie her jacket. Some kids on skis promised to search for her helmet and gloves.

After the girls warmed up by the fire, they got busy washing tables with Jeff and David. The foursome whispered their theories.

"Remember how nervous Mr. Johnny was last night in the store?" Jeff said.

"Yeah," said Sophie. "Like he was hiding something."

"And he said he'd be working on the chair-lift this morning," David recalled. "What if he saw Claire and Sophie coming and tore off the warning sign?"

"But why would he do that?" asked Claire. "He's not mean. He's just kinda —"

"Kinda guilty about something," said Jeff. "He likes brownies, we know that much, and probably potato chips. Maybe he forgets to sign out for his snacks up at the chalet. Last night he paid for his stuff in the market, so he's not a thief."

They looked out at the sundeck where the man was still on his cell phone.

"Maybe it's that guy," Claire said. "I don't think he likes us."

*   *   *

The children continued their discussion as they helped one another with brooms and dustpans. They took trash out to the Dumpster and brought in firewood. When they came into the kitchen, Miss Allen was hanging up her coat. She had just ridden up the lift without skis, like the tourists who come for lunch and to enjoy the view. In her white quilted vest she looked elegant, except for her frown.

"I hear there's been more trouble," she said.

"Miss Allen, we can explain —"

The woman held up her hand. "I know. It wasn't your fault." Her voice softened. "I'm just glad you girls weren't hurt. *Please* be more careful — all of you. If too many things go wrong around here, it could ruin business and the Zimmermans will fire all of us. Now, I've got some things —"

"Excuse me, Miss Allen," Jeff interrupted. "What does Mr. Johnny do when he works on the lifts?"

She gazed out the window at the hanging chairs moving slowly up the mountain. "My brother is in charge of maintenance," she replied. With a sigh she turned back to the children. "He's just sick over what happened today. He's been a caretaker here and at Camp Whispering Pines for twelve years, but nothing like this has ever occurred. Yesterday he noticed a problem with that chair and told a lift operator to put up a sign. Turns out the kid used flimsy tape, so it peeled off in the wind."

The children pondered this news. Then David said, "We saw him at the market last night. In the health food section. He seemed —"

"You did?" she asked. She glanced toward the pantry where there were shelves of canned food. Now Miss Allen seemed nervous. "I really do need to get to work. Make sure you kids have a nice hot lunch. It's sunny out, but the temperature is still below freezing."

After bowls of tomato soup and grilled cheese sandwiches, the foursome cleared their trays.

"Ready for the top of the mountain?" David asked. "We can race each other down to the bottom."

Sophie put on a knit hat that a ski instructor had given her to stay warm. "You guys can go ahead. I don't feel like riding another lift today. Maybe tomorrow."

"I'm with you," said Claire. "Let's head down to the Lodge. We can watch the ice rink, maybe rent some skates."

"Actually," said Jeff, "that sounds good to me, too. David, let's get our snowboards ready. We'll meet you outside."

The girls brushed crumbs from their table with napkins, then threw away their trash. While gathering their coats, Claire gave Sophie one of her gloves.

"So we each have a warm hand," she explained.

"Hey, thanks, Claire."

"Guys!" Jeff called, running back into the cafeteria. He was out of breath.

"What's the matter?" the girls asked.

"The snowboard Dad gave me. It's not on the rack. We've looked everywhere."

"What do you mean?"

"It's missing!" Jeff cried, his brown eyes watery. "Someone's taken it!"

8

Thin Ice

The children searched for Jeff's snow-board. They walked the snow-packed areas around the chalet and ski patrol hut. They checked the lost and found. They looked at every cluster of skis, poles, and boards that were propped against the sundeck and in racks. As the afternoon went on, the sun moved lower in the sky, casting the mountain in shadow. It was getting colder.

Jeff was starting to shiver. He wrapped his

wool scarf around his neck. "What if that man who was watching us took it?" he wondered.

"Or maybe someone else grabbed it by accident," Sophie offered. "So many of the boards look alike."

"Yeah, maybe it's already been turned in down at the Lodge," said Claire. "We should get going before the slope's too icy."

David put his hand on his brother's shoulder. "I'll ride down the lift with you," he said.

Jeff was too disappointed to answer.

That evening, dinner was at the Bridger cabin with Claire's parents. Aunt Lilly and Dr. Bridger were sisters and often planned meals together. This time they invited Sophie's family, too. The cousins' three dogs erupted in barks and wagging tails when the Garcias arrived with an apple pie.

"The map you drew us really helped," Mr. Garcia said to David. "You folks certainly live way out here in the wilderness. I didn't know the lake was so big."

"David is always drawing," Jeff said, proud of his younger brother.

Sophie helped the cousins set the table, then they went into the sunroom. The twins were on the couch with Tessie, the calm, old yellow Lab who liked to put her head on a cushion. But the two other dogs were too excited to settle down. Rascal, the Scottish terrier, and Yum-Yum, Claire's little white poodle, chased each other 'round and 'round the room.

The children didn't want their parents to worry, so they hadn't told them about the day's events. While waiting for dinner, David took out his sketch pad and rolled up his sleeves. His turtleneck was rumpled, having been under his bed all week.

Jeff's snowboard, he wrote by the list of missing items. Then to mark the unfairness of it, he added, *THE ONE DAD GAVE HIM!!* "Guys, we have to find it," he said, looking up.

"It'll take forever to earn money for another one," Jeff said. He wore a clean fleece, fresh from his drawer. His hair was brushed out of his eyes, unlike his brother, who often forgot to comb his.

"You can use my board!" said Claire. "We'll trade off."

"Mine, too," Sophie offered.

"Really?"

"Yep," Claire answered. "Besides, tomorrow Sophie and I are doing something different. We're taking Yum-Yum up to the chalet, to show Miss Allen. She wants to buy a dog just like her, to keep her company in her office. So we'll help clean the cafeteria and get lunch. Also, we're taking some games. If it's sunny, you'll see us out on the deck."

"That's so cool of you guys," Jeff said. "Thanks."

"I'm glad you can use my snowboard," said Sophie. "My parents won't let me go without a helmet. Anyway, back to our mystery, something weird's going on."

David chewed on the end of his pencil. "What if someone's trying to scare away the tourists? Or what if someone's jealous that we get a free lift pass?"

"We work hard for it!" said Claire. "We're not freeloaders."

"Well, what about those two guys in the control booth?" Jeff asked. "They were really mad they got fired. And they were mad at me and David for helping you guys off the chair."

David added *dudes that got fired* to his list. Then he said, "But if they took Jeff's board, we'll never find them, because they're gone for good. How about that man who yelled at us? Maybe he's trying to keep us off the mountain."

The brothers went to the wall of windows that faced the frozen lake. It was as flat as a white floor. Lost Island was in the dark distance, where the cousins' clubhouse was hidden among pine trees.

"I wish we could walk out there," David said. "We always seem to figure stuff out when we're in Fort Grizzly Paw or up in our lookout tower."

"Why can't we?" asked Sophie. "People are skating on the ice in the marina."

Jeff explained. "It's different out this far. The ice looks thick. But there are hot springs up the canyon that dribble warm water down into the lake here."

"Last winter we saw a moose fall through," Claire said. "At least he was close to shore and didn't drown. We don't dare try to walk to the island."

Sophie looked out at the black sky twinkling with stars. "It's so beautiful here. I just didn't know there was so much danger."

9

A Dark Sky

The next morning Jeff and David went snow-boarding. Claire and Sophie rode up the lift like sightseers, their backpacks and Yum-Yum's travel case on the seat between them. They each gripped the handle so the bag wouldn't fall over the edge.

Miss Allen welcomed the girls into her office. A couch was under the window where they put Yum-Yum's blanket and little teddy bear.

"I feel terrible about Jeff's snowboard," Miss Allen said. "I guess I overreacted about my watch and the other missing things. It's dreadful to think there's a thief up here." As she set a bowl of water on the floor for Yum-Yum, a gust of wind rattled the window. Suddenly, the sky darkened with clouds.

"That's odd," said Miss Allen. "The weatherman reported sunshine for today."

They looked out at the distant mountain range. A gauzy curtain seemed to have dropped from the sky, blurring the peaks.

"It's snowing over there, see, girls? Looks like it's coming our way."

Claire remembered the blizzards of last winter. After the boys' father had been killed, the cousins were extra careful about storms. They loved to snowboard in fresh powder, but

not in a whiteout. And not if there was avalanche danger.

They listened to the wind.

"I hope Jeff and David come in soon," said Claire.

By lunchtime it had snowed four inches. Only a few families were in the cafeteria. As Claire and Sophie washed tables, they kept glancing out the windows. Most skiers and snowboarders were passing the chalet, heading for the safety of town.

"You girls can leave if you want," said Miss Allen. "I've let the cook go home. He stocked the vending machines with sandwiches and fruit, so people can serve themselves."

"Thanks, Miss Allen, but we're waiting for my cousins," Claire said. "We always check in with each other. I know they'll be here."

"Okay. The lift closes at four o'clock. When you're ready to ride down the hill, take a blanket from my cupboard to put over your laps, so you'll be warm. I've already locked the kitchen door. Since you don't have a key for this one, just set the latch when you leave and it'll lock behind you. The fire will burn itself out. I'll see you tomorrow."

"Bye, Miss Allen."

The girls watched the falling snow. They played checkers and Boggle and old maid. They made a circle of dominoes on the table and let Yum-Yum sit in the center. The poodle was dressed up in her red ski patrol jacket that Claire had sewn, and a collar with a shiny bell. With her front paw folded under her chest, she kept an eye on the girls.

"I hope David didn't get wild again," Claire said. "He could get hurt, or hurt someone else. They were supposed to come in for lunch. Why aren't they here?"

By two o'clock, the families with young children had bundled up and left. The cafeteria was deserted. Snow swished against the windows, which were fogging up inside. The ski slope was a blur of white.

Just then, the door whooshed open with cold air. An older boy came in from the deck, his parka and ski hat covered with snow. A two-way radio on his belt crackled with static.

He was one of the workers from the top of the mountain.

"Well . . . well . . . well," he said, a sneer on his face. "If it isn't the troublemakers. My brother and his friend got fired because of you girls fooling around on the chairlift. We don't like kids who cause problems."

"What're you doing here?" Claire asked. She picked up Yum-Yum, who had started to growl.

"We're closing the lift early 'cause of the wind," he told them. "You better get going."

"We're waiting for our friends," said Sophie.

"Well, girlie, here's the news. The ski patrol has cleared the mountain, so no one else is up there. Like I said, you better leave."

The girls looked out at the slope, but there

was no sign of Jeff or David. "Maybe the guys are down at the half-pipe," Claire said to her friend. "We can go to my parents' café. That's where we always meet if we get separated."

"So you're leaving, right?" the older kid asked them.

"We'll get our stuff."

He spoke into his radio. "Tyler here. Lunch chalet is cleared. Over." He headed out into the storm.

The girls turned off the lights. While they zipped into their coats, they saw Tyler put on his goggles. Then he stepped into a pair of skis and pushed off with his poles, disappearing into the blowing snow.

Sophie's mouth dropped open. "He left us! Did he think we were skiing down? Who's going to help us onto the chair?"

"Well, he sure isn't!" Claire replied.

"What if they close the lift before we can get on?" Sophie worried. "And what if it stops *while* we're on it? No one will see us —"

"Then we've got to hurry," said Claire.

While they were putting Yum-Yum into her carrying case, a skier in black swooped onto the deep drifts of the deck. He cupped his hands around his face to peer in the window. Then he took off one of his gloves, pulled a key from his red fanny pack, and locked the door.

Before the girls could respond, he had skied away.

They ran to the front and shook the handle. The door wouldn't open.

"He trapped us inside on purpose!" Sophie cried.

Claire tried the handle again. Stomping her

foot in frustration, she said, "I bet he's the one who took David's key."

The girls rubbed the window to see out. To their dismay, they heard a loud *ker-thump* from the tower. With another *thump*, the motor shut down. The chairs were swinging from the cable, but otherwise they weren't moving.

The lift had stopped.

10

Alone

The darkened cafeteria felt colder than ever.

"No one but that awful Tyler knows we're here," Sophie said. She was close to tears.

The girls turned the lights back on, then went to the fire. The embers were low, so they added wood that was stacked against a wall. Soon they could feel heat from the flames.

Sophie wiped her eyes. "My parents are going to be upset when I'm not home by dinner."

"Mine, too."

"Let's climb out a window and start walking down the cat trail, okay? The lodge isn't too far. We can wrap Yum-Yum in an extra blanket —"

"No!" Claire cried. "My uncle taught us to never, ever go wandering in a storm. We're supposed to seek shelter and stay put. You and I are safe right here." She set Yum-Yum in Sophie's arms, knowing the little dog would comfort her friend.

"Here. You're in charge of keeping Yum-Yum warm. I'm calling my dad. Maybe they'll send a Sno-Cat for us."

Claire took her walkie-talkie from her backpack. After some clicking and static, her father answered.

"Are you all right, sweetheart? Over."

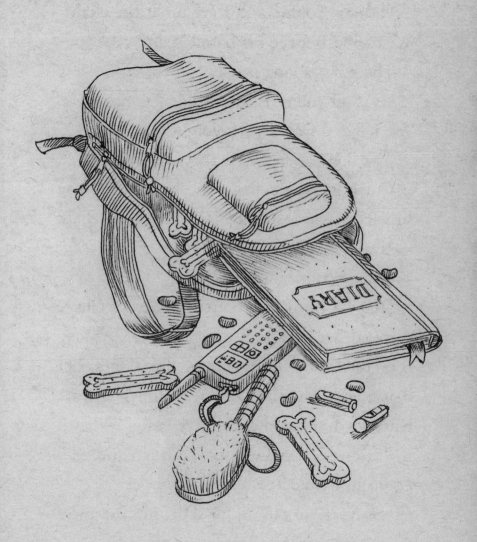

"Daddy, Sophie and I are up at the chalet. We're fine, but the lift has closed. Over."

There was a long pause.

". . . and you girls stay inside. Do not leave. Are Jeff and David with you? Over."

"We don't know where they are, Dad. Over."

Crackling came from the speaker, then a hiss. Then it was silent. Claire turned the dials.

"Daddy? Hello?"

There was no answer.

"Rats! I think my battery is dead." Claire emptied her backpack onto the floor. Among the clutter were jelly beans, dog bones, her diary, and a hairbrush. She found her spare batteries and put them in her radio. When it still didn't work she removed them and read the expiration date on their labels.

"I can't believe it, Sophie. These are supposed

to be good till next year, but they're duds. I've been ripped off."

"At least your Dad knows we're up here. And he'll tell my parents."

Suddenly, the lights overhead began flickering. The girls looked at the ceiling.

"What's happening?" Sophie asked.

More flickering, then the cafeteria went dark. Swirling snow at the windows cast a gray light. It was only three o'clock in the afternoon, but it felt like midnight. The wind's howling seemed louder than before.

"I think the power went out. Hold on." Claire felt among her belongings until she touched her flashlight. *Click.* Its beam reflected off a black pane of glass.

"Good!" said Claire. "I'm glad *these* batteries work. Let's look around."

They found the wall switch in the kitchen but the power was out there, too. The restrooms were dark. The hallways and kitchen were dark.

Rattle . . . rattle . . . rattle.

"Now what?" Sophie whispered.

"Sounds like the back door." Claire turned off her flashlight. The girls crouched beside the stove. When a shadowy figure passed by the window, Yum-Yum growled low in her throat.

"What if it's that man who locked us in?" said Sophie.

Claire started crawling for the pantry. "Come on, let's hide in here. Stay low."

The door rattled again.

"I wish we were in my parents' warm café," Claire whispered.

"Me, too."

Bump . . . bump . . . bump! Someone was kicking the door.

Claire and Sophie squeezed under a shelf, trying to make themselves as small as possible. They held tight to the growling Yum-Yum. "Shhh," they said.

Again the door rattled, then finally it banged open. In the darkness the girls saw two people covered in snow. The poodle managed to wiggle out of Sophie's arms and run barking through the kitchen.

"Hey, it's Yum-Yum!" cried a familiar voice. "Is anyone else in here, girl?"

When Claire snapped on her flashlight, she and Sophie gasped.

It was Jeff and David. Their faces were bloody.

11

Blizzard

"What happened?" the girls cried. "Are you all right?"

"We crashed into each other," Jeff explained. "It's so white out there we couldn't see."

Taking charge of her older cousins, Claire went to the sink with some paper towels. "You gotta wash up. You look gross."

David touched his cheek. When he saw the blood, he smiled. "Wow, we're messed up. We might have to get stitches."

"It's not funny, David," said Claire. "We've been worried."

She and Sophie helped the boys clean up. Their noses were bloodied, but none of their cuts needed stitches.

"Why didn't you get help from the ski patrol?" Sophie asked.

"We saw them, but we were standing in the trees," said David.

"No wonder!" their cousin said. "You're supposed to stay on the marked trails. The trees are out of bounds."

Jeff leaned into the sink to drink from the faucet. He dried his face with his sleeve. "Claire, we were dizzy from bonking into each other, so we went into the trees to get out of the wind."

"That's when we saw the ski patrol," said

David, "but they couldn't see us. We yelled like crazy, but they couldn't hear us either."

"So we called Mom on my radio to let her know we were headed here." Jeff held up his key for the back door. "Luckily, this was still around my neck."

The girls told Jeff and David about their afternoon.

"It was like Tyler left us up here on purpose," Sophie said. "The lift stopped right after he radioed someone."

"And that guy with the red fanny pack locked the door with David's key," Claire went on. "He even stared in the window at us."

"This is double weird," said Jeff.

"That's for sure!" David agreed. "At least I know where one of my keys went."

The children sat at the kitchen table, quiet with their thoughts. They shared bottles of apple juice from the refrigerator, and Claire's jelly beans. The storm continued to whistle and howl.

Jeff looked at his watch. "It's four-fifteen. We better put more wood on the fire."

"Are we snowed in?" Sophie asked.

"It's too dangerous for a Sno-Cat to come get us," the older boy answered. "We should prepare to spend the night. So, yes, we're snowed in."

"I'll get Miss Allen's blankets," Claire said, getting up from the table. "We can put her couch cushions by the fire."

"I've got a flashlight and a bag of chocolate almonds," David said.

Sophie felt cheered when she saw the cousins working together. "Hey, wait up, Claire. I'll help you."

By early evening, snow began to seep under the door. The children stuffed the cracks with mittens and ski hats from the lost-and-found box. It was getting colder by the hour.

The fire was in the center of the cafeteria and had four hearths. Against one of these hearths they arranged several benches turned on their sides, to form a large horseshoe. Then into the center they piled cushions and blankets, all their coats and sweaters, backpacks, and several camping pads the boys found in a closet. Since they would be sleeping on the floor, the benches would help keep away drafts. It would be a warm nest.

After this project, the children found the keys to the vending machine. They filled cafeteria trays with sandwiches, cookies, and fruit, then brought their dinner before the fire. Yum-Yum curled up by the girls.

"This is like camping with Mr. Wellback," Jeff said about their family friend. The elderly man was visiting relatives in Sun Valley. "He has lots of stories about Blue Mountain. I wish he were here."

"Me, too," said David. "Hey, that reminds me!" He brought out his sketch pad and pencil. "Let's work on our investigation. First off, we still don't know why Miss Allen and Mr. Johnny act like they have a secret. Second, what did we decide about the broken chairlift?"

"I think it was just a coincidence that we were on it," Claire said.

"Same here," Sophie agreed. "That leaves the missing items: two bags of potato chips, a brownie, and lunch things from the ski patrol lady."

"My snowboard," Jeff continued, "and Miss Allen's watch."

"We know about my key," said David. He added a big check mark by this drawing. "Looks like the only thing in common with all this stuff is that they disappeared from this chalet."

Claire ate some of her cheese sandwich. "Don't forget," she said after taking a sip of juice, "two people are mad at us: Tyler, because his brother got fired, and that skier because David was being wild. Maybe they want us out of the way."

Again the children were thoughtful. Warm light from the fire reflected off their faces. They didn't want to look behind them, at the shadows filling the cafeteria.

12

A Mysterious Print

All night the blizzard scoured the mountain. The children were cozy in front of the fire, but could not sleep. Jeff checked his watch every hour. At two o'clock in the morning they were still whispering.

A sudden light made them bolt up.

"The electricity is back!" David shouted.

But as the children blinked and looked around, they realized it was dawn. They had been asleep after all. The first rays of the rising sun were touching the mountain while the town of Cabin Creek was still in shadow.

They untangled themselves from their blankets to look out the windows. The drift was above their heads, so they stood on their tiptoes to see out.

"Wow!" cried Sophie. "The lift chairs are piled with snow, like giant marshmallows. It's so pretty."

Jeff grabbed his coat and gloves. "Come on, David. Let's start digging ourselves out of here. Two shovels are on the deck."

"Right behind you," his brother replied. Yum-Yum trotted outside with them.

Claire and Sophie brushed their hair into neat ponytails. Then they folded the blankets and returned everything to Miss Allen's office.

After straightening the benches, they tried the phone and all the light switches.

"Still no power," said Sophie. "At least sun is coming in the windows."

Coats on, the girls took brooms out to the deck. They swept snow off the picnic tables and chairs, and from the railings. Meanwhile Yum-Yum was rolling in the drifts. She wiggled on her back, kicking her legs in the air. She dug furiously with her front paws and growled, as if playing a game, then shoveled her nose through the snow. Her little bell was making so much noise that Claire removed her collar and set it on a table.

She called to the boys. "Sophie and I will get us all some breakfast. Ten minutes, okay?"

"We'll be there."

The kitchen was on the dark side of the chalet so the girls opened the door for sunlight. They set tuna sandwiches on the counter with four bags of potato chips. While pouring cups of cherry cola, they heard Yum-Yum barking and barking and barking.

"I wonder what's wrong," said Claire. She and Sophie hurried out front.

Yum-Yum was staring up at the picnic table. Her pretty bell was no longer there.

"Hey, David, where's the collar?" Claire cried. "We left it right here."

The boys looked out from behind a drift they'd been shoveling. "Huh?"

"You didn't take it?" Sophie asked.

"Why would we do that?" Jeff answered. He and his brother exchanged looks.

Claire threw her hands in the air. "How could it just vanish?"

The children stood in the cold sunshine, wondering. All around them, the snow was pure and white and glistening. Not even a rabbit had ventured out to leave tracks. There was no sign of any animal or human. And no sign of Yum-Yum's collar.

The girls glanced around the kitchen. Something felt different, but they weren't sure what it was. The door was still open. The plates and napkins they had arranged on the table were still there. The sandwiches and cola were on the counter as before.

"Didn't we put out four bags of chips?" Sophie asked her friend.

Claire nodded. "Yep."

"But there are only three," said Jeff. "What happened to the other one?"

The children looked out the back door. No tracks led to or from the kitchen.

"This is crazy," said Claire. "Two more things are missing, but we're the only people here."

"Hey, what's that over there?" Jeff asked, pointing to a small slope beyond the chalet. Carved into the fresh snow were strange marks, as if someone had sledded. But there were no footprints anywhere nearby.

David shook his head with bewilderment. "It's like an alien landed at the top of the hill, slid down, then took off in his flying saucer. Maybe that's why Yum-Yum was barking."

"You mean an alien took her collar?" Sophie asked. "Then when we weren't looking, an alien stole some chips?"

"Probably," said David.

"Wait a second, guys," Claire said. "Remember the other day when you threw a french fry to the birds? And a gray jay took off with it?"

"Yeah?"

"Maybe he's the food thief. I remember the kitchen was so hot that Miss Allen told me to open the widow over the sink and the door. The brownie and chips were right there on the counter —"

"Okay," said Jeff, trying to think logically. "Even if a jay came in for a little bag of chips, I doubt it could fly away with a brownie or Yum-Yum's collar. Those things are heavy.

And what about my snowboard or Miss Allen's watch —"

Loud crackling came from the walkie-talkie hooked to his belt. "Jeff, David? It's Mom. Please answer right away. It's an emergency. Over."

13

Emergency

The children crowded around Jeff. The girls held hands, fearful that something had happened to their parents or the little twins.

"Hi, Mom, it's Jeff. Are you okay? Over."

Static made it hard to hear her voice.

"... avalanche hit the Lodge ... chairlift is buried ..."

"Mom? Hello? Over."

"... Sno-Cats are needed in town.... Mr. Johnny ..."

"Mom, what happened to Mr. Johnny? Is everyone all right? Over."

Silence.

David, Sophie, and Claire looked at the older boy for an explanation.

Jeff's brown eyes were solemn. "I guess the slope above the Lodge gave way like last winter," he told them. "It'll take hours and hours for them to dig out." He paused. "I think we better bring in more firewood and get out the blankets again."

Now the children kept their worries to themselves. Last night by the fire, they had discussed the dangers of living in the mountains. Even experienced, careful forest rangers could get caught in an avalanche.

*   *   *

While Jeff and David shoveled a path to the ski patrol hut, the girls carried a tray of snacks outside. But it wasn't for lunch. They set a bag of chips on one table and a bag of miniature rice cakes on another. They put a ham sandwich in a pouch used by the ski patrol, closed its Velcro flap, then hung it from the railing.

"We might as well stay busy," Claire had said after the foursome agreed to set a trap for the food thief.

They waited inside the chalet by a sunny window. Jeff had found a book of western birds in Miss Allen's office, and was reading aloud.

"*Gray jays,*" he began. "*They're called camp robbers because they snoop around campsites and steal food. They live in the woods, mid to high elevations. They're not shy and are easy to tame.*

Sounds to me like they're brave enough to walk into this kitchen."

"I want to tame a bird," David said. "I hope one comes soon."

But only mountain chickadees fluttered down to the deck, no gray jays. Meanwhile, Sophie and Jeff played checkers. David drew in his sketchbook, Claire wrote in her diary. An hour passed. Drowsy from the sun, they lay their heads on the table. They were almost asleep when Yum-Yum gave a sharp bark.

The children looked outside to see a shadow hovering over a picnic table. It was a large black bird with shaggy feathers under its chin. It landed, and confident as a sheriff, it strutted over to the potato chips. It poked the bag with its bill, then hopped backward. It hopped side-ways, again poking to make sure it wasn't a

danger. Finally, it grabbed the bag in its beak and glided away on outstretched wings.

"What was *that*?" Sophie cried. "It's as big as a penguin."

Another black bird swooped down. It hopped and danced around the bag of rice cakes before flying away with it. When the third one landed at the ski patrol hut, the children watched in amazement. This bird sat on the railing, studying the pouch where the girls had hidden the ham sandwich. It jumped over it, cocking its head to see it from another angle. At last, it stepped onto the bag. Using its feet to hold it down, it bit the Velcro flap until it opened. The bird plunged his head inside, then flew off with the sandwich still in its baggie.

"Those crows have been spying on us!" David exclaimed.

Jeff was flipping through the book, shaking his head. "Uh, I've never seen crows that big before."

"Well, what are they?"

Jeff tapped a color photo. "Ravens. They're huge! They can grow up to twenty-seven inches."

"That's bigger than Yum-Yum," said Claire.

"Listen to this," said Jeff, again reading aloud. "*Ravens are related to crows, magpies, and jays. They mate for life and can live up to forty years. Experts believe they may be the smartest of all birds. Ravens have been seen leading a wolf pack to a prospective meal, so that the wolves will* expose the carcass and make it easier for the birds to eat the meat."

"Wow." David looked out the window. "That's pretty smart."

"What else does it say?" Sophie wanted to know.

Jeff continued reading. "*Ravens like to play and do aerial acrobats. They can mimic the human voice, even bark like a dog if they want. They're attracted to shiny objects such as coins and jewelry.*"

"The bell on Yum-Yum's collar was shiny!" said David. "And I set my key on that railing, remember?" He took out his notebook and began writing **robber bird** next to some of the clues.

"Poor Miss Allen," Claire said. "I bet a raven

stole her watch from the windowsill. How will we ever find it for her?"

"We still have more to figure out," Jeff reminded them. "I doubt ravens flew off with my snowboard. And we still don't know what Mr. Johnny and Miss Allen are hiding, or why that skier locked this cafeteria door. And what about those alien prints in the snow?"

Suddenly, David grabbed his flashlight. "Come on, guys. We might have one answer."

14

An Unlikely Suspect

Since the power was still out, David led the others through the dark hallway into Miss Allen's office. He shone his light on a bookshelf where there were several framed photos.

"See that one there?" he said. "When Jeff and I were looking for something to read, I noticed something familiar."

The children stared at a portrait of a ski team smiling at the camera. The skiers were wearing white racing bibs with a number and logo that said BLUE MOUNTAIN BEARS. A man standing in the center wore a black jumpsuit and red fanny pack.

"It's that guy!" Claire exclaimed. "Who *is* he?"

David's flashlight revealed other photos with skiers and this same man. Plaques on every one were from a different year and read: WESTERN REGIONAL CHAMPIONS WITH COACH ZEKE ZIMMERMAN, CO-OWNER OF BLUE MOUNTAIN.

"Zimmerman!" cried Jeff. "So this is who Miss Allen's been talking about. He's a coach and an owner."

"That explains why he yelled at David for being a maniac on the hill," Claire said.

"Makes sense," agreed the younger boy. "I bet he was telling those lift operators to yank my pass if I did it again."

Sophie was studying the photos. "He seems like a nice man in these pictures. Why would he lock us in the cafeteria?"

The foursome glanced around the office for more clues.

Finally, Jeff said, "I wonder about that window he looked in. Which one was it, Sophie?"

The girls went out by the fireplace. "There," they pointed.

Jeff went up to it and rubbed his finger along the glass. It squeaked from the moisture. "These aren't insulated," he announced. "See how fogged up they are around the edges where cold air leaks in? Our dad taught us about this."

"What does that mean?" asked Sophie.

David stepped forward. With his finger he drew a smiling dog on the glass. "It means," he said, "that the colder it is outside, the foggier these windows get. When Mr. Zimmerman looked in, he probably didn't see you guys sitting in the dark."

"Right," said Jeff. "And since he's an owner, he has his own key for locking up."

"So what about Tyler?" Sophie asked.

"He works at the marina in the summer," Jeff answered. "He's a rough guy, but he's not cruel. I bet Tyler didn't know you needed the chairlift to get down the mountain."

David took out his sketch pad. In the suspects' column, he put a check mark beside *Tyler* and *black widow spider skier guy.* "Two down, two to go," he said.

*　　*　　*

As the children gazed outside, they were startled to see a bearded man coming over the hill on snowshoes. He was wearing blue jeans with a rucksack on his back, and he was striding with poles like a skier.

"I sure hope that's Mr. Johnny," Claire sighed. She was suddenly tired of being brave.

15

A Visitor

Jeff was the first with his coat on and out the door. The others followed. Yum-Yum, in her red ski patrol jacket, bounded through the snow to welcome Mr. Johnny.

The caretaker planted his poles by the deck, then removed his snowshoes. A rolled-up sleeping bag was strapped to his pack.

"Thank goodness you kids are all right," he said. His beard was frosty from his long hike. "I left camp before sunrise this morning to make sure you're okay. The Sno-Cats won't be able to get up here till tomorrow. Your families are safe. In fact, no one was hurt in the avalanche."

Claire and Sophie hugged each other with relief.

"We're glad *you're* safe," Jeff said. He liked being the oldest and being responsible, but like his cousin, Claire, he was comforted that an adult was now with them.

Mr. Johnny took a two-way radio from his pack, much larger than the children's walkie-talkies. He pressed a button and was soon talking to Dr. Daisy Bridger. "The kids are in great shape," he reported.

Jeff and David were happy to hear their mother's voice. "Thank heavens," she said.

"We're standing by and we'll see you all tomorrow. Over."

David noticed another item on the man's belt. Mr. Johnny took it off and handed it to the younger boy. "It's an avalanche beacon. I carry it when I'm going back and forth up here. Just in case. It sends out a signal showing where I am."

"Maybe we should all have one," Sophie said.

"We already thought about it," said Jeff. "But they're really expensive. A couple hundred bucks at least. We just have to be super careful to stay on the marked trails and listen for warnings."

"Mr. Johnny, are you hungry?" Claire asked. Like her parents in the Western Café, she was a good host. "We can make you lunch."

"Thank you, Miss Posey. I'm starved and thirsty."

In the kitchen, the children set out sandwiches on the table with water. But before sitting down, Mr. Johnny went into the pantry. "Hmm," he said.

"Is something wrong?"

"I usually keep rice cakes in here," he replied.

The girls looked at each other. "We fed them to the birds," said Sophie. "We're sorry."

"That's okay," he said, now looking in the walk-in fridge. The food was still cold because the fridge door had been closed.

"Oh, good. Apples ‘and cheese and rice pudding."

"Here's a turkey sandwich," Claire offered when he joined them at the table.

"Thank you, dear, but I can't eat bread."

"What! No bread?" David asked.

"Food allergy," the man explained. "I recently learned that I'm allergic to gluten."

"What's that?"

With his pocketknife, Mr. Johnny sliced some apples to share with the children. "Put it this way, the only flour I can eat, without getting sick, is corn, potato, and rice. I have to read ingredients carefully."

"Can you eat brownies?" Claire asked. She remembered the cellophane and blue ribbon they found up on the path to Camp Whispering Pines.

"Not the ones they sell here." Then he smiled. "My birthday is coming up and my sister wants to bake me a special cake. She's been experimenting with rice flour. So far her corn bread is excellent."

"Is that why you were in the health food section the other night?"

Mr. Johnny nodded, but looked away as if embarrassed. "I'm sorry I was unfriendly. I guess I didn't want it broadcasted that I was buying special food, because I store it up here in the pantry. My sister and I try to keep it secret because the owner has accused us of wasting time. But honest, she only cooks for me when she's off duty."

The children nudged one another under the table. It was their way of agreeing they could trust Mr. Johnny. So they took turns telling him about the missing items and the ravens.

The caretaker threw his head back and laughed. "Well, I'll be. Those are smart birds, all right. Last summer, the forest service had to cut down a tree. We found a nest in the branches that had belonged to ravens. It was so well constructed that it didn't fall apart. Funny thing, there was a set of car keys and a bunch of pennies in it. You know how people don't bother to pick up pennies if they drop 'em? Well, the ravens are watching."

David opened his sketchbook. He crossed off Mr. Johnny and Miss Allen from the list of suspects. By the drawings of her watch and the brownie, he wrote **robber bird**. Then he tucked his pencil behind his ear. "That about wraps up our investigation," he announced.

"Except for my snowboard," said Jeff. "I guess a human stole it."

"You can use mine whenever you want," Sophie reminded him. "I still have to buy another helmet before I'm allowed to go out."

Jeff smiled at her. "Thanks, Sophie. Then let's trade off. When *you* are on the slopes, you can use my helmet."

"Hey, guys," Claire called from the sink, where she was filling the water pitcher. "You have to see this. Hurry."

16

Playing in the Snow

Mr. Johnny and the children rushed to the window.

"Shh," they said to one another as they watched an amazing event.

A raven was rolling down the hill, his wings tucked in at his side. His beak opened and closed as if laughing.

When the bird reached the bottom of the slope, he stayed on his back and wiggled, his feet straight up in the air. The feathers

around his legs resembled baggy, black trousers.

"Yum-Yum does that!" Claire said in her loudest whisper.

"This is so cool," said Sophie.

"It's awesome," Jeff and David agreed.

The raven now stood up, fluffed its feathers, then flew the short distance to the top of the hill. It found a fresh patch of snow and once again rolled over and over and over, down to the bottom. Legs in the air, it again wiggled and kicked.

"Why's he doing that, Mr. Johnny?" Sophie asked.

The man's beard moved up with his smile. "Looks to me like the bird is playing. It's a sign of intelligence when an animal can amuse itself."

"Where are his buddies?" Jeff asked.

"My guess is they take turns. Maybe they haven't finished eating your potato chips." Mr. Johnny laughed. "I wish I had my camera."

"We should let Yum-Yum out and see if they play together," David suggested.

Claire turned to him. "David Bridger! Are you kidding? That bird would probably carry her away and eat her."

"Sorry!" He threw up his hands and backed away. "I'm really sorry, Claire. It was just an idea."

"Hmph," she said, crossing her arms.

They continued watching until the raven flew away. He left behind more of the "alien" prints the children had noticed before.

Mr. Johnny gave them a mischievous grin. "It's a sunny day and we have nowhere to go. You kids want to build a snow fort?"

"Yes!" they cried at once.

"Okay, get your warm gear and we'll meet out front by the deck. We have extra shovels in the shed."

When Claire had zipped up her coat and found her gloves, she whispered to her cousins and Sophie. They nodded. The four-some crept out the back door and alongside the sundeck. They peered over the railing and saw Mr. Johnny carving a wall out of one of the drifts.

Without a word, the children made snow-balls, stacking them at their feet. Then with a nod, they began pelting the man's parka.

Plop . . . splat . . . splash!

But as calm as you please, Mr. Johnny reached for his own pile of snowballs.

"Fire, one!" he cried, and with bursts of laughter and sprays of snow, the five of them let loose with their ammo.

GET A SNEAK PEEK AT
JEFF, DAVID, AND CLAIRE'S
NEXT EXCITING ADVENTURE:

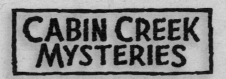

#6: THE SECRET OF THE JUNKYARD SHADOW

The Secret of the Junkyard Shadow

The tall oak swayed in the wind. High in its branches, twelve-year-old Jeff Bridger perched with his binoculars. The view was spectacular. Though it was spring, mountains in the distance were still white with snow. The surrounding forests were pale green with new growth. Jeff scanned the lake and its far shore that touched the marina. His gaze then followed the road that led past the café and the library.

At the edge of town, he focused on the junkyard.

"There he is again," Jeff said to his cousin, Claire, who sat beside him on their homemade platform.

"I see him, too," she said. Claire Posey

was nine. Her red hair blew around her face as she looked through her binoculars. She could read the DANGER signs on the barbed-wire fence. One showed a skull-and-cross-bones with the word POISON. Another sign said, NO KIDS ALLOWED, EVER, AND THAT'S FINAL.

"Is he carrying that suitcase again?" called David from the base of the tree. He was Jeff's younger brother, age ten, and today was in charge of delivering snacks to their lookout tower. The children's three dogs were wagging their tails as David fed them crackers from the torn bag in his hand.

"Yep, same as yesterday," Claire yelled down to him. "Wearing overalls and boots. Still can't see his face. He's hunched over in the shadows."

A creaking rope rubbed against a branch as it rolled upward over a pulley. A bucket soon appeared, clunking against the platform.

"Got it!" Jeff cried, leaning down. A lock of his brown hair fell over his eyes. He removed a carton of orange juice and the crackers. Claire made room on her seat for David, who then climbed up. The three zipped their sweatshirts against the cold air.

The cousins were on Lost Island, where their secret clubhouse was hidden in the woods. Their red canoe was tied to a log at the water's edge where they had beached it that morning. At long last, school was out for spring vacation. Now that ice had melted off the lake, they planned to paddle over from their cabins as often as possible.

"I heard the junkyard guy lives there in an old car with some pet tarantulas," Jeff said. He took a swig of juice, then passed the carton to Claire.

"We should investigate," she replied. She took a swig, then passed to David.

"Definitely!" the younger boy agreed. His blond hair was unruly in the wind. He gulped the juice, which spilled onto his shirt. Mopping it with his sleeve, he said, "I've always wanted to look around that place. I like junk. Wonder what kind of danger is in there."

"Maybe his tarantulas bite," said Jeff. "That's why he doesn't want kids around."

Claire finished a cracker, then picked up her binoculars. "And maybe they're poisonous. Hey, guys, check this out."

The brothers focused their lenses. They could see the man putting small objects into the suitcase. He strapped it shut, then heaved it over the fence. It landed in a puff of dirt. The man looked around and behind him as if hoping no one was watching. Then he crawled under the barbed wire, grabbed the suitcase, and ran through the woods.

The children set their binoculars down.

"If that's the owner, why didn't he go out the gate?" Claire asked.

"And it's weird that he put stuff in a suitcase," said David.

Jeff nodded. "Yeah. Whoever this guy is, I bet he's doing something he shouldn't."